JAMES TOWNSEND JR.

ALL MY LIFE I HAD TO FIGHT

DORRANCE
PUBLISHING CO
EST. 1920
PITTSBURGH, PENNSYLVANIA 15238

Dorrance Publishing Co
585 Alpha Drive
Suite 103
Pittsburgh, PA 15238
Visit our website at www.dorrancebookstore.com

ISBN: 979-8-8860-4101-9
eISBN: 979-8-8860-4017-3

ACKNOWLEDGMENTS

I would like to thank my mother for her love and how she understood how a young male can react while being on drugs in today's world. The making of this book wouldn't have come into effect if it weren't for the love of reading that was within my mother. Some days and nights, my mother would lay down in her king-size bed, and read for hours all the time. It happened so much that I would sometimes buy her different kinds of books to read. Mainly on "Mother's Day" or on her "Birthday," and just on other occasions. This acknowledgment also goes out to my uncles and aunts, also my brothers and sisters. There were even times in my life that my grandmother and my step-grandmother always thought that I wouldn't amount to anything in life. They all thought I was always bad even when I was good. To all of my kin, who really didn't know me that well, and because of their lack of interest in me. What they forgot to realize is that, I am a fighter and, "all my life I had to fight." Whether my fight was physical, mental, or spiritual, if it wasn't for the help of "Our Lord and Savior Jesus Christ," I don't know where or what I would be doing today in my life. He (Jesus Christ), has carried me a mighty long way within my life, even when I didn't know Him. Even while I am not totally safe, I am more than glad of His love for the "Backslider" … thank You Jesus!

"PJ" was a young man who grew up within two different kinds of family, whereas he had to go outside his beliefs, and his conviction of feelings. PJ first had to prove to himself before proving to his family, just because you're the black sheep of the family, you can't always be bad. He went through the love and mistreatment of being a stepchild, and at the same time fighting every day of life, living in the "projects." PJ learns that, down life-circle road, you can find out what love really is, when you get to know the meaning of, "love is, what love does." After also understanding what a man's duties are in life, PJ knows now that in life you don't have to fight all the time to get along with someone, especially when you learn and find out who Jesus Christ is. He also learned that feeling the presence of Jesus Christ is something that lives inside you, but it is totally up to you to seek His spirit and keep it. Life has a lot of ups and downs! PJ fell down and out in his life, but he never gave up. His story is what a lot of young men experience living in the projects! Out of all the fighting in his life, he finally learned to settle down. To this day, PJ's memories of his past still haunt him. They just will not go away!

CHAPTER ONE

On a cold winter morning, a young man is awakened by the sound of traffic coming through the window of his grandmother's house. He starts to think about what happened the night before. When he and his uncle, one of his father's brothers were enjoying themselves with some wine and smoking marijuana. With these thoughts in his mind, he put on some clothes, two pairs of pants, and two shirts. He starts to walk through his grandmother's house until he reaches the door, and while looking out the back door window, he has one thought within his mind—how to feel the same way as last night. "PJ" and his uncle were listening to music and enjoying the night. After spending the night, PJ woke up with the thought that there was a store down the street, two blocks from his grandmother's house.

By the way, this young man, whose name was Peter Johnson, was about 5'11" in height, and he had a slim build, and went by the name of PJ. His hair was dark brown, and his skin was the color of a Native American, who had been out in the sun hunting all day for something to eat. He was at the age of twenty doing this time in his life. PJ would sometimes live with his grandmother, on his father's side of the family. He normally stayed with his mother and his stepfather, along with six sisters and five brothers. But sometimes PJ and his stepfather would get into a big argument about helping out around the apartment. So, PJ would leave home and stay with his grandmother. Now PJ's grandmother was about 7 feet tall, and also had a slim build. Her children would call her "MaM."

She had nine boys and four girls, who all loved her very much. The reason PJ's grandmother has so many kids was because, back in the late '50s and early '60s, there weren't any birth control pills around. MaM had her first child at the age of fourteen, and now at this time in PJ's life, his grandmother was seventy-two years old. This was the same situation with PJ's mother. She had six boys and six girls, which were born, one right after another one, Ellen was the name of PJ's mother. She was short and one of the best cooks in the neighborhood. She came from a half-breed family, which consisted of, half African American and half Native American. Now PJ had one sister older than him and one sister under him. When PJ reached the store, which was two blocks from his grandmother's house, he had a plan in his mind. Before leaving, the idea of changing clothes after taking some money from the store cash box began more clearly.

PJ entered the store with two kinds of weapons and one was in his front right pocket, and another weapon was inside the bottom of his right sock. There were two customers inside the store. So, PJ began to walk around until those customers left. PJ came up to the counter, with his hand inside his pocket. The cashier, whose name was Don Jefferson, had moved to Alabama from New York. The reason behind Don's movement was because of the weather. Don was tired of the snow up north. He stayed with his wife, Joyce and their two daughters, Valarie and Janet. This was Don's first job in Alabama after five months of searching around. Joyce was an RN, who transferred from Bellevue Medical Center in New York to Jackson Hospital in Montgomery, Alabama. She was the bills overseer in the family.

When PJ approached the front counter, Don could see that look in his eyes. Don began to reach under the counter, where the store manager kept a .357 revolver. He pulled out the revolver with his right hand. Shaking with the .357 revolver in his hand, he said to PJ, "Get on the floor feller!" PJ looked at Don, and started to proceed to do what he said. Now Don was already suspicious of PJ's behavior. The thought ran through Don's head, that PJ was a young man who looked up to something. PJ didn't know the store had a silent alarm placed next to the .357 revolver under the counter. When Don was holding that weapon on PJ, he hit that silent button.

By doing so, Don knew that police would be on their way in less than fifteen minutes. Within twenty minutes, there were two patrol cars on the scene. While PJ was lying on the floor, one of the officers came through the door, with his relegated department handgun, held within his left hand. PJ heard these words, "Don't you dare move, nigger, or I'll blow your head off!" Officer Bob Mongreek was a down-to-earth country boy from Memphis, Tennessee.

He came to Alabama seven years ago. He was medium height, and a middle-aged guy, with salt-and-pepper hair. His belly stuck out as if he had been drinking a lot of beers every night after work. He lived on the east side of town, where most of the middle-class people lived. Now when Officer Bob put the handcuffs on PJ, and brought him to his feet. The other officer stormed through the door to assist Officer Bob. Jim O'Malley was the name of the other officer. Officer Jim O'Malley was an Irishman, whose relatives came to America in the late '20s. But Jim was raised in Alabama, after his family moved from Chicago in 1964. Jim had a wife, and her name was Mary. Officer O'Malley searched PJ's pockets and his shoes for more weapons before putting him into a patrol car.

"Well, is he clean?" asked Officer Mongreek.

"Almost, he had an icepick in his sock down his right leg! Damn, what was he planning?" Officer O'Malley wondered aloud.

"Okay let's take him downtown and get him booked," said Officer Mongreek. "I'm hungry. I forgot to eat breakfast this morning."

CHAPTER TWO

PJ was raised in the projects on the north side of the city of Montgomery, Alabama. There were over 300 people staying in these projects. The projects were very dangerous back in the late '60s and early '70s, so dangerous that it was once called, "a bucket of blood!" All the older people would say that evil spirits would walk throughout the projects. They said this because there was a graveyard across the street on the west side of the projects, and that entitled projects was once a cemetery. Many people, young and old, have died in these projects. PJ's family would always have to move to a bigger apartment complex because PJ's mother kept having one baby after another. So, they continued moving until they reached the largest apartment around. There were four rooms that contained three bedrooms upstairs, and one bedroom downstairs, next to a large living room. It also had a big kitchen. Growing up in the neighborhood was very tough for PJ and his brothers and sisters.

There is nothing in the world like living in the projectss at the age of seven and up. But PJ was just one of those kids that experienced projects life from kid to adult. PJ's father was once in the Army, and PJ was born on a military base in North Carolina. PJ's mother and father were from Alabama. Peter Johnson Sr., joined the military when he was sixteen years old, and met Ellen M. Slaughter in high school. They lived a happy life while in the military, until they returned back to Alabama.

Once arriving at the city jail, the officers took a vote on who is going to do the paperwork on processing PJ into lockup. But they both knew that both of their signatures are required; it's a company policy. A voice hollered out, "When can I make a phone call?" It was PJ, coming around to his senses. Two other officers placed PJ inside a small cell and removed his handcuffs.

A few minutes later, Officer O'Malley took PJ's fingerprints and also his mugshot picture, while the other officer did the paperwork.

"He's a skinny fellow!" said Officer Bob.

"Yeah, he is," said O'Malley. "What makes today's kids do these crazy things in the world, Bob?"

"Well, O'Malley, it all depends on the father and the mother. If they're not willing to spend any time with their kids and teach them the right way of life," said Officer Bob.

When PJ got through with his fingerprinting and having his picture taken, he was allowed his one phone call. So, he called one of his father's brother, whose name was Horace.

"Hello, Unc, I did something very stupid this morning," said PJ.

"What happened," asked Uncle Horace.

"I was so high last night when I went to sleep, I started dreaming up this idea about how to get some drugs and wine." PJ proceeded to tell his uncle what happened. His last two minutes came up on the phone.

"You have two minutes left," said the operator.

"While I am in this city jail, tell my dad where I'm at," said PJ. Uncle Horace was one of PJ's father's brothers. He would always try to keep up with all the younger guys in the family. He was 7" feet tall and slightly bowlegged. Uncle Horace loved the game of basketball and played for different teams in his lifetime. He had one bad habit and that was smoking marijuana. Likewise with his brothers and a couple of his sisters. Uncle Horace at the time stayed with his mother, in the center of the projects. Their apartment is where all the business of the projects flowed through. Well nevertheless, Uncle Horace couldn't get in touch with PJ's father. So, PJ had to stay in jail for two days before going before the judge.

"Hey, unlock cell door D of the hole!" a voice yelled out.

Okay," a guard answered.

PJ woke up to a rewarding day. It was time to go before the judge. After entering the courtroom, PJ starts to look around. He got a big surprise when he spotted his mother and his oldest sister along with one of his brothers.

At the end of the hearing, the judge ordered PJ to be mentally evaluated, after hearing the nature of the crime. So, this meant that PJ had to stay in jail a little longer. Judge Tyrone Carter, was medium height and weighed about 285 lbs., and had gray hair from his head to his chin. He had attended college at Stanford, but graduated from UCLA. One day, on a cold Monday morning, Judge Carter was about to arrest a man for an assault case, when all of a sudden, the man jumped out of his seat and tried to attack the judge. Fortunately, the jailer caught him before he reached the judge. After this incident, the Honorable Judge Carter would keep a small handgun inside his robe. The man was sentenced to two years in the city jail. The man's name was Alexander Hills; he was from Miami, Florida.

One day while visiting Alabama, Alexander was confronted by a man about some money. This man just walked up to Alexander, and asked him, "Where is my money?"

Alexander replied, "What money and who are you?"

The man replied, "The money you borrowed from me two weeks ago!"

"I'm sorry, sir, but you have the wrong guy," said Alexander.

"No, I don't," said the man, we were at a bo-layer's house on the north side of town, drinking!" After saying that, the man reached for Alexander with his fist closed tightly and tried to punch him. Alexander ducked down low and spotted a Coca-Cola bottle on the ground. He proceeded to pick up the bottle and hit the man on the right side of his head. The man went down and started to holler. As he was falling, blood started to flow down his neck onto the ground. At the same time this incident was going on, a police patrol car was passing by, and the officer spotted what was going on. Alexander was placed under arrest.

This caused Alexander to get so mad, that when he went before the judge, his anger came out at the judge. So, he tried to attack the judge. The judge sentenced Alexander to two years in the City Jail. While taking off, the judge yelled out, "Maybe you'll cool off while doing that time, young man!" The jailer placed Alexander into the same cell with PJ. Alexander began to introduce himself, but PJ wasn't listening. He was thinking about an incident that happened in the past. PJ had an adventurous past that was deeply rooted in the way he was raised. In his thoughts, he went back to the age of fourteen.

At this age, PJ had his first job with his stepfather. He assisted his stepfather in a customer cleaning service, which consisted of cleaning floors and restrooms, taking out the trash, and shining floors. Other thoughts ran through his mind about how things were before the job, when living in the projects and selling drugs at the age of fourteen. The older guys of the projects were kind of drawn to him, because of how tough PJ was, so they showed him how to hustle and make money fast. Which included gambling with dice, playing pool, and selling drugs.

At this time also, a well-known pool sharp opened a pool hall in the neighborhood, and noticed how PJ was so interested in shooting pool. He also liked the way PJ carried himself. This pool sharp was named "Big Buster." He was from New Orleans, but was raised in Detroit, and weighed around about 305 lbs., and stood about 6'2" in height. Buster liked PJ so much that he gave him a job managing the poolhall while he was out. PJ was very excited and now he had two jobs. PJ was the youngest poolhall keeper in his town and also in his neighborhood projects.

CHAPTER THREE

All of a sudden, a loud noise threw PJ's thoughts off. It was Alexander hollering at a floor-boy for a cigarette. Back in the late '70s and early '80s, every lockup, whether it be the State Prison or even the County and City jjails, there was always a trustee (or back in the day called a floor-boy). When Alexander received his cigarette, he proceeded back to talking to PJ.

"So, PJ, what are you in here for?"

PJ didn't want to tell him the truth, so he said, "Old tickets." PJ waited a couple of minutes and asked him the same question. "What are you in here for?"

"Well, young blood," said Alexander, "I'm in here for an assault, but it was in self-defense. Man you have got to be careful in these streets. A guy thought I was someone else that he was looking for."

PJ replied, "Yeah, I know about the streets. I grew up on one of the toughest projects around this part of town. This projects used to be called 'Bucket of Blood.'" PJ kept on talking about the projects to Alexander. The reason people would call this projects "Bucket of Blood" is because it was built on top of a graveyard. Many had died in this projects. PJ recalls to Alexander about seeing a guy get shot over a penny dice game. This young guy goes by the name of "Fast Eddie." That terrifying day, Fast Eddie was gambling with this older guy named "Willie Pete."

The two guys started an argument over who won. The argument got so serious that Fast Eddie pulled out a small .22 revolver and shot Willie Pete in the left arm. After being shot, Willie Pete jumped up and started to run. Fast Eddie shot a couple more times at Willie Pete while chasing him. The shots were so close that Willie Pete could hear the bullets passing by him. The projects had a big park located in the center, where everyone would go and have a good time. It had a basketball court, and a set of swings with a medium-size monkey bars, and a big field, for football and baseball. You can see in every direction at the opening of the park. This made it easy to see when the police were coming.

Willie Pete was so busy trying to get away from those bullets Fast Eddie was shooting, he forgot about trying to get into someone's apartment. All of a sudden, he saw someone's door open. Now this projects was built with two doors in front and one in the back. The front had a screen door with a hard door connected, and locks. Willie Pete saw this door opening and tried to get into it for safety. When all of a sudden, PJ heard a loud gunshot from another direction. It came from the apartment of one of PJ's friends, Wes Johnson. Wes was a very "cool" guy, kind of big, and had a very dark look about himself.

He always wanted to be a pimp when we were growing up. Wes had just stepped out of his mother's apartment while everything was going on. Wes was headed to the park and Willie Pete saw him leave his mother's porch. So, he proceeded to go to Wes's mother's porch. Wes's mother was in the doorway at this time looking around to see where the gunshots were coming from. When she saw Willie Pete coming to her porch, she got scared. She quickly ran to her closet and reached for her son's gun, which was a .45. When Willie Pete reached her door, he got shot in the chest by Wes's mother and died there on the front porch.

Everybody gathered around and started looking. This was the first time PJ saw a dead man. While listening to PJ, Alexander was blowing smoke around the cell and was about to fall asleep. So, PJ got silent and started to do some more thinking to himself about his past again. The conservation he had with Alexander stirred up his memories, so he went back to the age of eighteen. At that age, PJ was a smooth dresser and he always wanted to be a businessman. After learning some street ways from the older guy in the projects, PJ felt that dealing drugs was not the way to go all the time. After a year had passed by (still in his deep thoughts), PJ remembered getting a job on the west side of town, at a package store. This package store was called "JJ Lounge."

This store would stay open from 9:00 a.m. until 11:00 p.m., Monday through Saturday, and on Sunday it would be closed. PJ, after closing, would sometimes have to walk home from the west side of town to the projects on the north side of town. On the way home sometimes, he would stop at a McDonald's restaurant, which was set on top of a hill. This McDonald's was a block away from PJ's job. One Saturday night, PJ met a couple of guys at McDonald's, who asked him if he smoked marijuana? With that question upon him, he said yeah. So, these guys, who were brothers, and were from the countryside of the county, were passing through.

They often gave PJ a big sack of marijuana for a low price. PJ brought it and took it home and rolled it up to smoke. PJ couldn't only smoke half of that rolled up marijuana, because of the effect he started to feel strange. PJ explodes into a ten-day nonstop sleeping experience. His head gave him the feeling of beginning from another world, and thinking that he had the power of a god. With each growing day, PJ felt stranger and stranger, as if he were growing taller and taller by the minute. When these things were going on within PJ's mind, his mother became very worried, knowing something was not right with her son. So, she asked one of her brothers to take PJ and her to see a doctor. But her brother said no, therefore she had to ask one of PJ's father's brothers because his father was nowhere to be found.

Charles was one of PJ's father's oldest brothers, and was well known for being creative with things, things like, brick work and setting tile. When PJ and his mother and his uncle reached the hospital, the doctor evaluated PJ and recommended that PJ should be committed to a mental place for some help because of the drugs in his body. The doctor had determined that PJ had smoked a rare form of marijuana called, "PCP." Which is better known as Angel Dust, a mind-blowing drug or known as, horse tranquilzer. PJ's mother didn't let him know that he had to be committed. The day PJ and his mother arrived at the hospital, PJ didn't know it was a mental hospital. He just thought he had to be evaulated again. His mother asked him to sign some papers and unaware what was going on, he signed the papers. Afterward, while PJ's mother and uncle were talking to the doctor, PJ began to wander around the place. He starts to look out of a window. He noticed a big green field, and started to think to himself, how nice it would be to walk around that field.

So, he walks to a door and attempts to open it, but it is locked. He tried another one, unfortunately it was locked, so he headed back to where he left his mother and uncle, up front at the information desk. But they were not there, PJ began to look around. At that moment PJ got mad, so when he was feeling like this. The orderlies (which consisted only of males), tried to calm him down. They couldn't calm him down, PJ began to run and they couldn't catch him. He went through a door, which was a bedroom with a window. He began to try to get through the window that he saw, but unfortunately every window and door he tried was locked. PJ ran into one more bedroom, and tried another window, but it was locked also, at the same time, the orderlies were chasing him.

The orderlies tried to grab PJ, but they couldn't, because PJ was fighting with his feet and fists. He was swinging and kicking. He managed to get out of that bedroom, and was running down the hallway. PJ got cornered at the information desk. When this happened, one of the orderlies caught PJ from behind while he wasn't looking. The orderly pushed him down into a chair, then other orderlies reached under the chair that PJ was sitting in, and shot him with a needle into the chair. Now that needle contained a medication made for sleeping. PJ started to feel weak, the orderlies was able to push PJ while he was in the chair. They pushed him down the hall into a room with walls made of rubber. When PJ starts to realize what they were trying to do, before going into the room, PJ grabs the entrance walls, but was unable to overcome the orderlies. They closed the door real fast and PJ's two largest fingers on his left hand were caught in between the door entrance and the door. They closed the door so hard, that the door was cutting into PJ's fingers. Blood begins to run down PJ's hand onto the floor. One of the orderlies saw the blood on the floor and quickly opened the door. He opened wide enough just to let PJ's fingers out. PJ was in great pain, but there was nothing he could do.

While PJ was thinking about his past, Alexander, who was sitting on the side of his bed across from PJ, asked him a question.

"Are you okay?" asked Alexander.

PJ replied, "Yeah, just thinking about something that happened in the past. This happens every time I look at my two largest fingers on my left hand. I think about the damn hospital that I was committed to for a crime I had committed."

"What hospital was that?" asked Alexander.

"It was something that happened to me, that such have never happened. And besides I don't want to talk about it!" After going back into his past and having that conversation with Alexander, PJ started thinking and feeling that the cell he was in couldn't hold him. He started grabbing some sheets and pillow cases, and began to tie them together. Thinking he was skinny enough to get through one of the cell windows. But unfortunately, one of the inmates, who sweeps and mops the floors was thinking another way. This inmate thought PJ was trying to hang himself, so he called the guard. When the guard came back to PJ's cell, PJ didn't see him because he was too busy trying to tie those sheets and pillow cases together.

The guard, whose name was Jack, hollered out at PJ, "Mister, what are you doing?" PJ turned around and looked at him, and could not say a word. Jack opened the cell door and reached out at PJ, grabbing him by his arms and proceeded to take him out of the cell. PJ was placed into a single cell, which was called solitary, or "the hole." This cell consisted of a concrete floor with a hole in the center of the cell. There was no bed, and it had a small sink and no mirror. PJ had to take off all of his jailhouse clothes because the system didn't want any inmates to be a threat to themselves.

Two hours had passed, and PJ had gotten a visitor, it was his court-appointed lawyer. The guard took PJ and his court-appointed lawyer into a small room, so they could go over the case. After talking to his lawyer, the lawyer considered that PJ was under the control of some kind of drug. And, therefore, his case was an act of insanity, and that PJ should be mentally evaluated. So the lawyer told PJ that he was going to put in a plea of "not guilty by reason of insanity." Now PJ wasn't really listening to his lawyer, because he was wondering why the guard didn't give him any clothes to put on. After talking to his lawyer, PJ was put back into his cell. And was held there until he had to go before the judge, which was within four days.

Jack the guard, woke PJ up and said, "Okay, young feller, it's time to see the judge. Here, put these clothes on!" When PJ finished putting his clothes on, he and Jack passed Alexander's cell. All of a sudden, PJ hears a voice saying, "See you around, youngblood!" It was Alexander, standing up in his cell watching them. PJ just looked at him and nodded his head. Once in the courtroom, PJ begins to look around. He was surprised to see his oldest sister and their mother, along with one of his brothers. The judge was an old man with salt-and-pepper hair, his name was, the Honorable Judge Ricky Williams.

Judge Williams was very tall, about 6'4" and looked to weigh about 275 lbs. Well, it is hard to tell his exact weight because of the rob he wore. The judge looked at PJ and then stared down his lawyer and said, "Let's get started." PJ's court-appointed lawyer's name was Joshua Hamilton. He was a Florida boy, who was short and had a German Shepherd dog for a roommate. The state prosecutor was a medium-build lady, who goes by the name of Tina Franklin. After hearing the case, the judge ordered PJ to be mentally evaluated at a mental hospital, and remain there until he is fully evaluated. The name of this hospital was Bryce Mental Hospital. It was a place known for housing all types of criminals for every type of crime.

The judge didn't give PJ a length of time, but stated that he'll have to stay until he is fixed for another trial. When PJ arrived, he didn't fully understand where he was or why he was there. This was because some of the effects were still in his body. While riding around the hospital campus, PJ saw people walking around in their pajamas and wearing T-shirts and some people wearing jeans. They were walking around as if they had places to go. PJ and the guards came to a tall building. The criminally insane were kept on the tenth floor of this building, inside a locked gate. This floor contained a locked porch with a see-through fence. This is where inmates were allowed to go and smoke, or just to catch some fresh air.

PJ slowly began to come to his senses and thought to himself, *only in the movies does a place like this exist.* It was hard for him to believe. After a couple of weeks, PJ starts to feel lonely. The thoughts of his family kept running through his mind. But he realized that life must go on. Time was passing by fast, and after three months, PJ got his first visitors—his mother and one of his sisters along with two brothers, and his mother's sister's daughter. When greeting each other, some of the male security guards automatically liked PJ's sister and cousin. Anastasiya was a pretty young woman for her age, which was seventeen at the time.

Now Anastasiya would carry herself with a lot of class, as if she were a Hollywood star, which was very different from living in the projects! PJ's cousin's name was Sonja. She was PJ's mother's favorite sister's daughter. She was fifteen at the time, and had the beauty of a magazine model. The security guards pulled PJ to the side, and asked him, could he introduce them. There were only two security guards to each shift at a time. One of the guards' name was Robert Harris; he was about 6'2", and had a dark complexion. The second security guard was named Michael Thompson; he was short, about 4'9". His coworkers would call him "batmice" because of his height.

When PJ realized that the two security guards liked his sister and cousin, he began to bargain with them. He asked them if they would bring him some small amount of marijuana. If so, he would get his sister and cousin's phone number for them. So, the bargain was made. Both Robert and Michael would bring the drugs and leave it under PJ's mattress. This would happen once a week, while everyone was outside in the recreational area. This idea of PJ's had turned out well. He planned to sell each rolled-up marijuana stick for $5.00 each. But only to the inmates that he could trust.

After some months of being at the mental hospital, PJ would hide his money from the sale of drugs, outside on the porch, where they go and smoke cigarettes, inside a hole in the wall. He had it wrapped up inside a sock. In the seven months of his lockup, PJ had to return to the city to face trial again. PJ arrived in the courtroom, walking through the door like a zombie. With both of his arms struck to his side while he walked. PJ was looking straight ahead as if he were in a trance. When the judge saw this, he quickly committed him back to the mental hospital for more evaluation. No one inside the courtroom or at the hospital knew that PJ had planned this scene. This was in order not to be sentenced for the crime he had committed. Once PJ returned back to the hospital, he put in a request for a job around the hospital campus. After receiving a job moving old furniture out of patients' bedrooms, and replacing them with new furniture. So, with the money from the job, PJ no longer had to hide his money from the marijuana. He just combined all his money together into a savings account.

CHAPTER FOUR

After fourteen months, before PJ's time was served out. He was taken off medication, to see how his reaction would be. After he calmed down, he got into a couple of fights. One fight began with one inmate from Detroit, whose name was Winton. Winton refused to let PJ pick someone on his team, while playing basketball in the recreational area. Now Winton was a big guy with one eye and he wore an eye patch on one eye. Before PJ and Winton got into a physical fight, the security guards stopped them. The second fight started, when PJ was trying to protect an inmate that was a friend. This inmate was from Birmingham, Alabama, and his name was Bobby. Bobby and Winton didn't get along. Because of the incident, each inmate was placed into a locked room, separated. It was once again time for PJ to head back before the judge. It had been twenty months being evaluated, and the judge heard about PJ's fights.

So the judge ordered PJ to be sentenced to two years in "T-Town" (which was Tuscaloosa). He had to attend a rehabilitation center, because of his tender. The judge also stated that PJ wasn't to come home within those two years, and classified him as a "menace to society." Once in the Rehabilitation Center, PJ shared a room. He had to show the doctors and counselors that he was capable of handling his anger. After a couple of months in the Center, PJ was given a maintenance job at an apartment complex. Where he would cut grass and pick up trash daily.

One summer morning, while picking up the trash at his job. PJ spotted one of the most beautiful girls in the world, riding in a "T-top Monte Carlo" car. After seeing this young lady, the first thought that came into his mind was that she was going to be his wife. PJ learned her name from one of the tenants around the apartment complex. Her name was Melvina McCoy. She was short around 4'11", with long hair and a beautiful light skin complexion. She lived with her mother, four brothers, and one sister. Every morning for the next two weeks, PJ would see her when she took her brothers to school. One morning, PJ built up his nerve to say something to this short, beautiful lady. He waited until she was coming back home from taking her brothers to school, and he walked close to her apartment. When she approached, PJ said hi!

"Hello," she replied. All of a sudden, she asked PJ, "You're not from here, are you?"

PJ replied, "No, I'm not!"

"I've seen you watching me," Melvina said.

PJ started to look pale. He always thought that she wasn't interested in him. "You are a beautiful lady," said PJ.

"Thank you," she replied. Where are you from?"

PJ said, "I'm from 'Monkey Town (which meant Montgomery, Alabama). Have you ever been there?" asked PJ.

"No, I've never been there before," Melvina replied. "As a matter of fact, I've never left this town!"

After all these questions, PJ asked her out, and she said yes. From that day on, the two fell deep in love and had a baby girl. They named her after PJ's mother, Ellen Shanna. The years passed on, and PJ's first two years with Melvina gave him the idea to take her home to meet his side of the family. Once there, things didn't turn out right. Are first six months at home, PJ and his girlfriend broke up. They both went their separate ways. Melvina returned home, and PJ moved in with his mother, until he found a place of his own. One hot summer day, one of PJ's brothers got into a fight with his girlfriend's friend. Now PJ's brother caught his girlfriend talking to some guy. So, they got into a big fight, and the information got back to PJ's mother's house.

Then all of a sudden, all of PJ's brothers ran out of the house, and found PJ's brother fighting with a guy from another projects. PJ's brother was named Ben, and the guy he was fighting was Bill. Ben and Bill went to the same school, and were about the same age. And now they wanted the same girl. Bill had been talking to PJ's brother's girlfriend behind his back. When the brothers caught up with the fight, all of the brothers jumped in. One of the brothers tackled the guy to the ground. When seeing him go down, PJ reaches into his pocket and brought out a pocketknife. PJ was about to cut this Bill, when all of a sudden, he hears a voice, saying, "Mister please don't hurt him!"

When PJ looked toward that voice, he realized that it was PJ's brother's girlfriend, and he pulled back. And everyone stopped fighting, because the other brothers were looking at PJ and wondering what was going on! Right then PJ told his brothers what he had heard, and told them that this relationship wasn't good. Everyone let Bill go and PJ told his brother, Ben, she doesn't love you anymore! Afterward life went back to normal. After this incident, PJ fell in love with a younger woman. Her name was Virginia; she was about 5 feet tall and had the same complexion as PJ. The years went by, and PJ moved in with Virginia. They had three kids, two girls and one boy, and lived on the west side of town in another projects. PJ got a job being a tile-setter helper, with one of his father's brothers.

The money wasn't enough for PJ to keep his family going, so he got involved in selling drugs again. Now this was in the early '80s, just when the movie *Scarface* came out, and everyone was into cocaine. After two years of dealing with drugs PJ decided to get out, and got into cooking. He worked two jobs, one was dealing with cooking, and the other job was still working with his uncle. This uncle was the same uncle that took PJ and his mother to the hospital, yes, Uncle Charles. Uncle Charles never finished high school, but always had the ability to build things. Being a country boy while growing up, he learned a lot of outdoor things. One day PJ and Uncle Charles were doing some work out at Montgomery Regional Airport.

They were building a new restroom floor and walls. PJ was asked to get some fresh water to wash off the tiles with. The water was cut off on the inside because of construction going on. This meant that PJ had to go outside and dip a five-gallon bucket into fifty-five drums of water. After doing this for three hours, PJ's last trip to the water drums affected him. When he dipped that five gallon into the fifty-five-gallon drums, he pulled up with his back instead of his legs. He hurt the lower part of his back, and was unable to work for five years. Now being in this condition, PJ had to go back to dealing with drugs full time, in order to support his family. During his last days of not working in five years, PJ got a summons for a court appearance. This was for late payment of child support. During those five years, PJ had applied for disability for his lower back pain.

This pain had caused PJ to walk around with a cane. Another one of PJ's father's brothers had gone to prison for two years for unpaid child support. So, this summons was heavily on PJ's mind. This uncle's name was Herbert, and he had let PJ know about his case. So, PJ was very nervous when he went before the judge. When he was called up front, PJ had to leave his walking cane behind. With that in mind, a young prosecutor asked the judge, "Your honor, if he can stand up here, he can flip a burger." The young prosecutor's name was Warren Pope. He appeared to be 5'9", and had a light-skin complexion. The judge asked PJ did he apply for disability?

PJ replied, "Yes, Your Honor!"

"Well now," said the judge, "Do you have your kids included on your disability application?"

"Yes, sir," said PJ.

So, Judge Ricky William, told PJ, that he had to finish paying the main amount of his child support, and that he was not to pay any more interest amount. When all this was over, PJ got a good cooking job as soon as his back felt better. After his relationship took a turn with his last baby mother, which he had swindled up marrying and divorcing after six years. They had been together for eighteen years. By now PJ's first girl, that was by his first relationship, had grown up. One holiday evening, PJ's big girl came down to visit her daddy. But all of a sudden, PJ's wife and oldest daughter got into an argument. It got so loud that PJ had to pull his wife to the inside of their place because PJ thought the argument would lead to a fight.

So, he started to pull his wife inside their place. When pulling his wife inside, she started to fight PJ. Saying that, PJ was taking her side of the argument. She starts biting on PJ and pulling some of his hair out. PJ broke loose and departed from their apartment. He didn't return to his family for some years. PJ's oldest daughter had met a guy and moved in with him. PJ didn't know until after that evening of the fight. So, PJ moved on with his oldest daughter, she had an extra bedroom. PJ maintained his cooking job for ten years. Often, he would sit in his bedroom and think about his past life. One thought that always comes to his mind is, when he first found out who Jesus was.

PJ had just turned seventeen years old, when one day his mother's youngest sisters told him about a church where the pastor would lay a hand on you and things happened. PJ asked her (Joyce) what do you mean?"

Aunt Joyce replied, "Demons and bad habits come out of you! And when this happens, your body would feel different. The church has a tarry service on Wednesday nights and Bible study on Tuesday nights, and the regular service is twice on Sunday. So, PJ, who always had these feelings that there has always been a higher power in this world that existed. Attending a Wednesday night tarry service at his aunt Joyce's church turned out to be more than an everlasting memory and feelings. At the beginning of the service, we started out singing and after that the bishop asked, "Would anyone here like to receive a blessing or healing from the Lord?" PJ stood up and began to walk toward the bishop, who was standing before the altar of the church. When PJ got in front of the bishop, the bishop asked him, "Do you believe in Jesus?" As soon as PJ said yes, the bishop placed his right hand on his forehead, immediately a feeling came over PJ and he fell to the floor. All PJ could remember was a bright light all around him.

While this light was surrounding him, a feeling hit him that he couldn't explain. But he felt so different and he thought he was on his feet, but all the time he was lying down. When he came to, everyone told PJ that he was talking in a different language.

"I never seen a light that bright before," replied PJ, "and I want to see it again." So, when PJ left the church, he came home and locked himself in his bedroom. And began to tarry the way he did at church. With his eyes closed tight and calling on the name of Jesus while slapping his hand together. After two minutes, that light appeared before him again. And immediately he felt very light off his feet, as if he were being lifted off his feet from the floor. When that light left PJ, he felt like a brand-new person. PJ's heart was renewed and he saw things in life differently. What he meant by different, was that his mind and body were feeling carefree.

After living the life as a Christian through his teenage years, PJ unfortunately backslid. PJ's past life kept on creeping up on him and he became weak, and let the Lord Jesus Christ down. PJ came back to his present mind of thinking, and sat alone in his room. Still to this day, he always keeps the thoughts of the existence of God to be real. Today PJ is still fighting inside his mind and this world-way of living!

9 798886 041019